Bailey
Goes Camping

By Kevin Henkes

Puffin Books

FOR LAURA

PUFFIN BOOKS
Published by the Penguin Group
Viking Penguin Inc., 40 West 23rd Street, New York, New York 10010, U.S.A.
Penguin Books Ltd, 27 Wrights Lane, London W8 5TZ, England
Penguin Books Australia Ltd, Ringwood, Victoria, Australia
Penguin Books Canada Ltd, 2801 John Street, Markham, Ontario, Canada L3R 1B4
Penguin Books (N.Z.) Ltd, 182–190 Wairau Road, Auckland 10, New Zealand

Penguin Books Ltd, Registered Offices: Harmondsworth, Middlesex, England

First published in the United States of America by Greenwillow Books, 1985
Published in Picture Puffins, 1989
By arrangement with William Morrow & Company, Inc.

10 9 8 7 6 5 4 3 2 1

LIBRARY OF CONGRESS CATALOGING IN PUBLICATION DATA
Henkes, Kevin.
   Bailey goes camping / by Kevin Henkes.   p.   cm.
   Summary: Bailey is too young to go camping with the Bunny Scouts,
but his parents take him on a special camping trip—in the house.
ISBN 0–14–050979–8
[1. Camping—Fiction. 2. Rabbits—Fiction.] I. Title.
PZ7.H389Bai 1989   [E]—dc19   88–24626   CIP   AC

Printed in the United States of America
by Lake Book Manufacturers, Melrose Park, Illinois
Set in Bookman Light

Bruce and Betty were Bunny Scouts.

They were going camping.

Bailey had to stay home.

"I want to go camping," said Bailey.

"You're too little to go," said Bruce.

"But in a few years you can," said Betty.

"Don't feel bad, Bailey," said Bruce. "It's
not *that* great. All we do is eat hot dogs
and live in a tent and go swimming and
fishing and hunt for bears and tell ghost
stories and fall asleep under the stars."
"And don't forget roasting marshmallows,"
said Betty. "That's best of all!"

Bailey watched Bruce and Betty leave.

"It's not fair," he said.

"Come on," said Papa, "let's play baseball."

"No," said Bailey.

"Want to help me bake cookies?" said Mama.

"No," said Bailey.

"We could read a book," said Papa.

"No," said Bailey. "I want to go camping."

"You're too little to go," said Papa.

"But in a few years you can," said Mama.

"Don't feel bad, Bailey," said Papa. "It's not *that* great."

"Oh, yes, it is," said Bailey. "You get to eat hot dogs and live in a tent and go swimming and fishing and hunt for bears and tell ghost stories and fall asleep under the stars. And best of all, you roast marshmallows."

"You know," said Mama, "you can do
all those things right here."

"I *can*?" said Bailey.

"He *can*?" said Papa.

"Yes," said Mama, smiling.

That afternoon, Bailey ate hot dogs

and lived in a tent.

He went swimming

and fishing.

That night, Bailey went on a bear hunt

and told ghost stories.

And best of all,

he roasted marshmallows—

before falling asleep
under the stars.